D033232

Text and illustrations copyright © 2001 by Mireille Levert
English translation copyright © 2001 by Groundwood Books
First paperback printing 2002

All rights reserved. No part of this book may be reproduced, stored in a retrieval system
or transmitted in any form or by any means, without the prior written permission of the
publisher or, in the case of photocopying or other reprographic copying, a licence from
CANCOPY (Canadian Reprography Collective), Toronto, Ontario.

Groundwood Books / Douglas & McIntyre
720 Bathurst Street, Suite 500
Toronto, Ontario M5S 2R4

Distributed in the USA by Publishers Group West
1700 Fourth Street
Berkeley, CA 94710

We acknowledge the financial support of the Canada Council for the Arts, the Ontario
Arts Council and the Government of Canada through the Book Publishing Industry
Development Program for our publishing activities.

National Library of Canada Cataloguing in Publication Data

Levert, Mireille
An island in the soup
"A Groundwood book".
ISBN 0-88899-505-9
I. Title.
PS8573.E956355I84 2001   jC813'.54   C2001-904285-X
PZ7.L5748Is 2002

Printed and bound in China by Everbest Printing Co. Ltd.

An Island in the Soup

Mireille Levert

$6.95

A Groundwood Book

Douglas & McIntyre Toronto Vancouver Berkeley

VICTOR of the Noodle, grand knight of the Order of the Macaroni, was bravely battling in the forest when he heard his mother call, "Supper!"

There on the table sat a bowl of the strangest fish soup, steaming suspiciously.

"Eat, Victor," said Mum.

He shook his head. "What you are asking is very dangerous, because in that soup, on that crust of bread, there's a…a…"

"An island in the soup!" exclaimed Mum.

"I'd have to cross a bubbling, cheesy swamp full of huge, stinky fish. Look at them jumping! Look at their creepy, pointy teeth!"

"How awful! Quick!" called Mum. And she held out a soup spoon.

Victor jumped aboard the boat.

"Watch me," said Victor. "I landed on the island and didn't even get my feet wet."

"Hooray!" shouted Mum. "You made it."

"But, oops," whispered Victor. "Listen to those eerie whistling noises."

Suddenly a rain of giant peas and carrots came crashing down on the poor boy. "Help," he shouted. "I'm going to be squished."

Mum pushed Victor under the table.

"Hide, brave knight," she said. "The storm will pass."

Poor Victor's legs were trembling. The rain of peas and carrots continued for a while. Then there was silence.

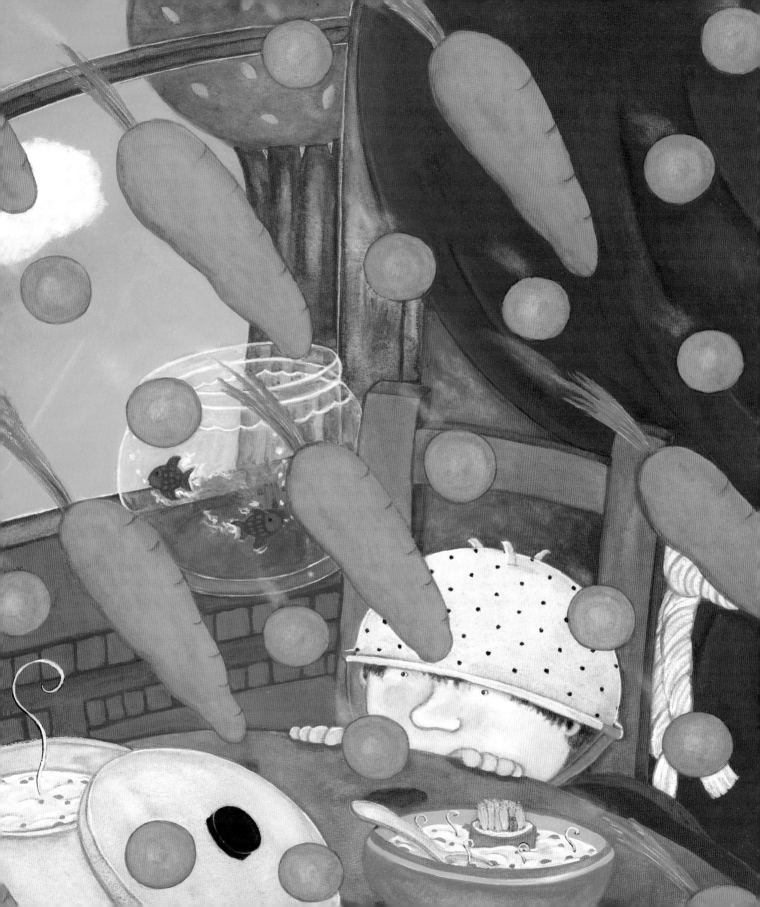

"You just escaped that time," sighed Mum.

Victor climbed out from under the table. "No, listen. Mum, can't you hear those leaves rustling? This forest of giant celery is being whipped around by a wild wind. I can barely see. I don't like all these creaks and groans in the dark. Mum, I'm scared!"

"Be brave, my knight," said Mum, and she handed Victor a lighted candle.

As Victor marched forward, he began to feel warm.

"A…a…achoo!" he sneezed. Big drops of sweat appeared on his face.

"Mum, I'm melting, I'm burning, I'm roasting. Look, a…a…a…choo! Oh, no, now it's a pepper dragon."

"Run, run," shouted Mum. Victor took off as though he were on fire.

He ran and ran until he reached an open door and dashed through, slamming it shut behind him. Too late he realized that he had foolishly entered the castle of Bad Fairy Zoop.

"Victor, where have you gone?" he heard his mother calling in the distance.

"M…um, I'm lost."

The words were barely out of his mouth when Bad Fairy Zoop grabbed him. "Ooh, a little boy," she grinned. She tied him up and started to tickle him. "Eat, little boy. Why won't you eat your fish soup, naughty thing?"

Victor shrieked, "Help, Mum, help! The bad fairy caught me!"

"Hold on," called Mum, "my lovely boy, my bunny, my chick." She flew to Victor's rescue, bellowing, "I'm the queen of the woods." Floating triumphantly over the boiling swamp, she glided easily between the flying peas and carrots.

Bing, bang! She dispatched the dragon by pouring water on his fire. The dragon skulked away, whining. Up again and she was off to Bad Fairy Zoop's castle.

As she rushed down the hall, Victor could hear her steps.
Zoop was insisting, "Eat, eat, eat your soup, naughty boy."

Victor was turning green. His head was spinning. He could
barely whisper, "Mum," as he gulped down the soup.

Mum leaped at Zoop. First she tickled her, then she lassoed
her. Before Zoop knew what was happening, she was upside
down and spinning around.

"Watch out, Zoop. From now on you'd better behave," said
Mum.

Victor and his mother went behind the castle, where they
found…

a most beautiful garden. A chocolate pool lay surrounded by a marzipan rose hedge. Beside it, under a huge pear tree, was a majestic table where two plates of the finest porcelain held two large pieces of cake, all ready to eat. On a little place card were gold letters that spelled

TO PRINCE VICTOR AND HIS QUEEN.

BIBLIOTHEQUE DE VILLAZARE

Suddenly, Victor was starving. He slurped up his soup, which had become cool. To his amazement, it tasted better than any soup he had ever eaten.